The Tiny
String of Pearls

Written by R. Barbara Fay
Illustrated by Jim Stahl

Edited by Chanté McCoy

shamrock

ISBN 1-886991-03-0

shamrock

For Kristin, Kevin and Kyle:
May all of your dreams come true.

One

An early morning rain pelted the bedroom window.

"Oh, no!" Kristin groaned as she rolled over, pulling the comforter over her face. Kristin had plans for the day: a bike ride to the park, swinging on the swings, maybe even a picnic lunch. And in the afternoon, her mother had said they might go to the zoo. But who would want to do any of that in the rain? Maybe it will stop, she thought, as she sat up and pulled aside the curtain. The sky was gray, and the window pane was splattered with heavy raindrops. Probably not, she decided as she let the curtains fall back into place.

Downstairs, her younger brothers were already eating breakfast.

"Good morning, Kristin," Mama said, greeting her with a plate of scrambled eggs.

"Good morning?" Kristin asked, taking her place next to Justin. She thought this morning was anything but good.

"It is kind of dreary, isn't it?" Mama agreed, sitting beside Geordie and helping him scoop a spoonful of eggs into his mouth. He giggled and pointed to the window.

"Rain, rain!" he babbled and clapped his hands.

"I don't know what you're so happy about," moaned Justin. "I wanted to play outside."

"That is exactly what I wanted to do!" grumbled Kristin, the two shaking their heads in shared misery.

"Oh, come on, you two," Mama scolded. "It's not that bad."

Kristin knew this was true. Worse things could happen. But, for the moment, she was very disappointed.

"It's so boring inside. There's never anything to do," she said.

"Your morning might be busier than you expected," Mama replied, smiling as though she could foresee some marvelous pastime that they had overlooked. "Your rooms are a disaster. Kristin, I'm afraid I discovered your hiding place for all the things you were supposed to put away for the past three months when I looked under your bed for a shoe yesterday. I'm surprised the legs of your bed still touch the floor! How much stuff is under there?"

Kristin giggled nervously and shrugged.

"Well, you should go through that mess to find out if there is anything worth saving. And after that, the bathroom needs to be cleaned, and the dishes need to be put away…"

"Okay, okay! We'll stop whining!" Kristin interrupted, recognizing the trick Mama used when she and Justin complained about having nothing to do.

"Thank you," said Mama, "but whether you are whining or not, you still need to clean your rooms. Then I'm sure you will discover all sorts of creative things to do to make this rainy day worthwhile."

Kristin nodded as she swallowed her last bite of breakfast. She then cleared her dishes from the table and trotted up the stairs to face her messy bedroom.

Two

Kristin's room was worse than she realized. How could it get so bad so fast? Justin must come in and play with her toys and leave them around, and then Geordie must follow him just to mess things up!

Unhappily, Kristin realized she could not blame her brothers. She surveyed the heaps of clothes and the piles of toys. The t-shirts and jeans were hers, and she remembered playing those games with Meghan, and building dollhouses from books and blocks with Kayla, and coloring those pictures and dumping those puzzles all by herself. Tidiness was not a part of Kristin's lifestyle, she had to admit. And this time, she really must put everything away where it belonged. With a determined sigh, she dove in.

First of all, she lumped the dirty clothes into

a laundry basket. Then she arranged the books on the bookshelves, stacking the puzzles and the games neatly beside them. Crayons were sorted and dolls were dressed and her comforter was pulled up over the rumpled sheets.

Next, Kristin investigated the collection of junk under her bed. She felt like Mary Poppins pulling surprises from her magic carpet bag. And what discoveries she made! She found long-lost game pieces and her stuffed kitty. She found remnants of Easter candy, her favorite pink nightgown, and what must have been her mother's missing shoe. She found old gum wrappers and more than a couple mismatched socks. And, in the back corner, face down in a pile of frothy dustballs, was her Ginghy-doll.

"Ginghy!" Kristin whispered, pulling her from the gloomy depths and carefully brushing the clumps of dust from her porcelain face and her tangled red-brown curls. Kristin traced her finger along a fine crack that ran from the doll's hairline down between her painted eyebrows, angling off the small nub that made up her petite nose, continuing down her cheek like a tear. Kristin remembered and felt sad. She hugged the doll to her chest, and her mind flew to the day that Geordie was brought home from the hospital.

There were many visitors that day. Melanie's mother brought banana bread, and Ashley's mother brought fresh fruit. Kayla's mother brought a beautiful blanket, and Katie's mother brought a stuffed bear. Everyone cooed over little Geordie and took turns holding him. Everyone, that is, except Kristin. With all of the adults around, Kristin was never given the chance to hold her baby brother. She had only touched him once at the hospital, when he had wrapped his wrinkled pink fingers tightly around her own much larger one. Since then, she had not even seen him up close! When she tried to squeeze between the huddled admirers to get closer, Meghan's mother bent down next to Kristin, and spoke to her seriously.

"Kristin, now that the new baby is here, you have some big responsibilities," she said as she pulled a video from her handbag. She handed it to Kristin as though it held rare, important secrets. "Here you go. Now you be a good big sister and take Justin downstairs to watch this movie while your mother gets some rest."

Kristin longed to stay upstairs to be with the baby. She looked at the adult faces, hoping someone would ask her to stay. But they all nodded in agreement with Meghan's mother. Even Mama, her face puffy and tired, did not object. So Kristin found Justin and together they went downstairs.

The house became quiet after the guests left; there were only the sounds from the television turned low and the *chop chop chop!* from the kitchen as Grandma fussed about preparing dinner.

Suddenly, the stillness was pierced by a high-pitched squeal from upstairs. The baby was crying! He was crying and crying, and nobody seemed to pay attention!

Kristin hustled up the stairs and found her mother's bed empty. Next to the bed, in a little wooden cradle, thrashed an angry Geordie, his face red and his chin quivering. His tiny baby shrieks were just heartbreaking. Kristin bent down to pick him up. He was heavier than she imagined, and his arms and legs flailed, and his little body squirmed. Before she could get a really good grasp, he twisted his head to one side and threw his legs to the other and his body wiggled from her arms!

Kristin remembered the whole scene so clearly. She could still feel her heart stop as his little body flipped and fell, and she could still hear her own shriek as she saw the edge of the cradle just inches from where his head would hit! And then, from nowhere, two hands came up from behind and caught the baby, just in time. They were old hands, wrinkled hands. Grandma's hands.

"He sure is making a fuss, isn't he?" asked Grandma, with no scolding or anger in her voice as she cradled Geordie in the crook of her arm. "Let's bring him over to the rocking chair and settle him down."

Grandma sat down and pulled Kristin onto her lap. They held the baby together, gently rocking as Grandma hummed her favorite lullaby while Kristin sang along.

"Hush-a-bye, don't you cry! Go to sleep little baby..."

Geordie's crying slowed to a whimper and then died away as his little eyes shut and he fell asleep. Mama walked into the bedroom, tying her bathrobe.

"What happened in here? Geordie was sleeping, so I decided to take a quick bath. I got out as quickly as I could when I heard him cry."

"Don't worry," Grandma whispered. "Kristin and I have everything under control."

Mama looked pleased and gave Kristin a kiss. "Thank you, honey. You really are a big help." Mama laid down and fell asleep almost as quickly as Geordie had. Grandma and Kristin placed Geordie back in his cradle and quietly left the room.

"Come with me to the kitchen," smiled Grandma. "I have something for you."

There, sitting at Kristin's place at the table, was Ginghy-doll. Ginghy had been Grandma's doll when she was a little girl. Whenever Kristin visited Grandma, she wished she could play with the doll, but it was breakable, and Kristin was too little. Ginghy was a beautiful doll, though perhaps a bit old and musty. More important, Ginghy had been Grandma's.

"Kristin, you are big enough now to have Ginghy-doll. I want you to have her, because I know you will take good care of her. But remember, she is very fragile. Just like a real baby, she can break."

Kristin thought about Grandma's words and touched Ginghy's face again. Then a sharp bang at her bedroom door brought her back to the rainy morning.

Three

"Aren't you done?" Justin called as he and Geordie burst into Kristin's room.

"Yep," she answered, propping Ginghy on her pillow. "I finally am. Let's think of something to do. I'm tired of cleaning."

"Sure," Justin said, "What do you want to do?"

"I don't know."

"How about play house?" Justin suggested.

"Nah," said Kristin.

"School?"

"This is the weekend. I don't want to think about school!"

"Trucks?"

"Nah."

"Blocks?"

"Uh-uh, I don't want another mess." Kristin made a face as she watched Geordie pull a block from the stack and put it in his mouth.

"Well, what should we play?" Justin asked again, looking frustrated.

"I know," she brightened, "How about hide-and-seek?"

"Yeah! I want to be 'It'!"

"Okay, Justin, count to twenty—no, you'd better make it thirty. I'll take Geordie with me. Remember to count loud!"

Justin hid his eyes and began to count. Kristin took Geordie's hand. In it was the slobbery wet block he had been chewing on.

"Yuck, Geordie," she cried, and quickly grabbed his other hand.

"ONE, TWO, THREE..."

The two tip-toed out to the hall, Geordie singing his "ABC's" and Kristin, eyes opened wide, searching for the perfect hiding place.

"...EIGHT, NINE, TEN..." they heard from her room.

"Come on, Geordie, we need to find a good spot!"

"Good spot!" he agreed.

They snuck into mama's room. Kristin looked under the bed. Although it was clean, it was too squishy under there for two. Behind the dresser might have worked, but it was too heavy, and there were bottles of perfumes and creams sitting neatly on top that would tumble off with a great crash if she tried to move it.

"...SIXTEEN, SEVENTEEN, EIGHTEEN..."

"Oooo, we better hurry!" Kristin said. Geordie had wandered over to the closet door and was pulling at the knob.

"Shoes! Shoes!" he said, reminding Kristin how he loved to wear Mama's shoes around.

"Good idea, Geordie!" Kristin quietly pulled the door open, and Geordie toddled right in. "Come on, we have to get way in the back."

"...TWENTY-EIGHT, TWENTY-NINE, THIR-TY! READY OR NOT, HERE I COME!"

"Shhh, Geordie. We have to be very quiet," Kristin whispered.

Minutes passed, and all the hiding pair heard was the rustling of the dry cleaning bags that fluttered with their breaths. Kristin's eyes began to wander along the shadows of the dresses and shirts and pants and skirts all hanging at attention. She glanced up to the shelves, scanning the round boxes and the square boxes and the old magazines and— what was that? There was something sitting high on the tallest shelf, something she had not seen before. She spotted it in the dim light,

as anyone might sense a hidden present: a tiny
box wrapped in dainty flowered paper tied
with a delicate yellow bow. It hung high above
her; she could not reach it or touch it. Kristin
knew right away that it must be a prize for a
very special person, like someone who could
do triple-flips off the balance beam or swim
fifteen lengths of the pool without taking a
breath. Kristin could do none of these fantastic
things, but she still wondered about it. For
whom could it possibly be?

Right then, she heard padded footsteps outside the closet. The door was flung open and
bright light streamed in from the bedroom.

"I found you!" roared Justin, proudly.

"Uh-uh..." answered Kristin, not really caring, much more interested in the lovely gift
peeking through the boxes above her head.
She stared at it, she wondered about it, and
she thought about it. She knew her birthday
was coming, and yellow was her favorite
color, so it really, truly could be for her.

Four

Kristin checked Mama's closet daily to make sure the hidden treasure had not been moved. She felt very sneaky, not like before when all she wanted to do was to touch Mama's dresses, count and sort her high-heeled shoes into "pretty" and "old" piles, build a fort with Justin and Geordie, or try on Mama's silky bathrobe. No, now she felt different. Kristin was quite certain she was not supposed to see that special something in the closet, and, if she were caught, she might find out it was for someone else. So, as quietly as petals fall from a flower, she would open the door and peer at the distant yellow-ribboned mystery box for just a second, as long as she dare. Then she would close the door briskly before hearing Mama's footsteps coming around the corner.

Kristin was edgy. she had never been very

good at keeping secrets. Her thoughts and feelings were always right there, if not in words spilling from her mouth, then in the smiles that spread on her face when she wanted someone to think she was still angry, or in the tears that brimmed from her eyes when she wanted no one to know that she cared. When Grandma had given her Ginghy, the whole neighborhood had probably heard her squeals of excitement. Knowing about the treasure in the closet was one of the few secrets she ever kept from Mama. The first one was about dropping Geordie. The second was about Ginghy...and Grandma.

Kristin could never have kept a secret from Grandma.

"I know what you're thinking, little dear," Kristin could hear Grandma's sweet, gentle voice. "It's in those beautiful blue eyes."

Whether it was how many twos Kristin had in her hand when they played Go Fish, or how she did on her spelling test at her school, or how badly she wanted to hold her new baby brother, Grandma always knew. And no matter what, Grandma always answered with a soft word, or a chewy cookie, or Kristin's favorite, a warm hug. If Grandma were here,

Kristin would have bubbled over about the hidden present right away. But Grandma was not.

A few months ago, Grandma had been sick. Mama had done all she could to care for her. Mama was gone a lot, and even when she was home, she was often crabby. One evening, Mama returned from a visit to the hospital. With swollen eyes and a weak voice, she told Kristin Grandma had died. Kristin did not understand. There must have been a mistake! How could Grandma be gone? Grandma would never leave her!

Kristin was furious. She ran to her room and slammed the door. She threw her toys hard on the floor and pounded her bed and screamed into her pillow. Then crossed her arms and sat. And sat. And sat. While Kristin sat, her anger cooled and peeled away, leaving a new emotion, raw, deep, and painful. She felt sorry about throwing her toys and picked them up. At the bottom of the pile was Ginghy.

Kristin's heart cringed when she saw the fresh crack scarring her Ginghy-doll's face. She could not look at it. She decided to hide Ginghy so perhaps she could forget, both about hurting Ginghy and about Grandma.

That was how Ginghy had made it to the hidden world under Kristin's bed.

Later that night, while Kristin tried to sleep, Mama came in and sat beside her. The room was dark except for the moonlight that shone through the window onto Mama's pale face. Kristin could see that Mama was tired and sad. Mama said she felt like there was a big hole in her heart. Kristin knew just what Mama meant, for she sorely felt it too. It would take some time to heal, Mama added, and then the memories of Grandma would bring warm smiles instead of hurting tears.

Kristin hoped this was true. She decided to keep her second and third secrets from her mother. She would not let Mama know how much she missed Grandma and she would not let Mama know about her breaking Ginghy.

Five

Finally, it was the night before Kristin's birthday. No big party was planned for the next day—maybe just some cake, Mama had said. Kristin understood why it would be hard to have a party. It just seemed like Grandma should be there. Having no birthday party did not matter, anyway. The excitement she felt for the secret package perched on Mama's closet shelf made up for missing a silly old birthday party.

Just to remind herself of the wonder of the mystery gift, Kristin decided to visit it one last time. She opened the closet door, as she had done every day, and looked up. Her eyes knew the spot exactly, but something was wrong. The present was gone!

Horrified, she ran to get a chair and dragged it into the closet. She climbed up and pushed aside old magazines, baskets, her Kindergarten art project, and a box full of old pictures, but found no mystery present. Where could it have gone? She tossed aside a hat box, a few musty books, and a rattly old jewelry box. Still no luck. It must not have been for her after all! Her heart felt as empty as the closet seemed, and she choked in the dust cloud her rummaging had created. She turned around on the wobbly chair, almost falling as she coughed, and then she gasped. Mama was standing there, her hands on her hips and her face very stern.

"Kristin, what on earth? Get down right now! Look at the mess you've made!"

"Oh, Mama, I was just looking," her eyes stung, and she squinted to hold back the tears.

"Kristin, you know better than to be tearing through someone else's things. And you could have been hurt, standing on this rickety chair. Come on, let's pick up this mess."

Mama reached up and started shoving things back onto the shelf. Kristin wanted to yell "Be careful!" just in case the delicate box was still up there, for if it was, it would surely be squashed. But Kristin was afraid she would give herself away. She never should have wished so hard for that present. It felt like nothing good could ever happen again! Mama kept talking:

"I just looked in your schoolbag and saw that you have homework to do. You'll want to get that done so you can go outside to play. It will be bedtime soon and you will have wasted all of your playtime snooping around my closet shelves!"

"Yes, Mama," Kristin answered, looking curiously at her mother. Even though the words she spoke were angry, the sound of Mama's voice was not. And the little wrinkles around her eyes were slanting upward, hinting at a smile.

Mama turned to Kristin and touched her fingers lightly under the young girl's chin. Looking at her daughter's sorry frown, Mama's face softened into a full, knowing grin.

"Oh, little Kristin, were you looking for this?" Mama's hand fell into her pocket and pulled out the magical mystery gift, its yellow ribbon even more beautiful than it had looked from afar. The wrapping paper was like Mama's summer garden, decorated with yellow roses and tiny pink and peach buds with

fine green stems and leaves. On it was a tag:
To Kristin, From Grandma.

"Oh, Mama, from Grandma? But she's…"

"I know, Kristin," Mama said quietly.
"Grandma bought this for you for your birthday. I'm sorry she isn't here to give it to you
herself. Why don't you open it?"

"Today?" Kristin asked, not believing.

"Uh-huh," Mama nodded.

"Right now?" Kristin asked again, amazed
that the moment had finally arrived.

"Yes, silly. Go ahead!"

Kristin carefully peeled back the enchanted
ribbon. The paper fell away easily, like a
flower blooming to share its secret inside, and
Kristin held a small, white velvet box. She lifted the lid and inside was a fine gold chain
strung with nine tiny glimmering pearls.

"Oh, Mama, look! A tiny string of pearls!"
Kristin whispered as if the necklace were
made of dandelion fluff that would blow away
if she spoke too loudly. "I love it! It's so pretty!
May I wear it?"

"Kristin, it is lovely, but it is also very fragile.
I don't think you should wear it this evening.
Why don't you wait until tomorrow? How
about when you have your cake? We'll all

dress up. It will be very special!"

"Oh, Mama, please? I can't wait! I'll take good care of it. Please?"

"Well, okay. But be very, very careful."

Mama placed the tiny string of pearls around Kristin's neck and hooked the delicate clasp.

"You look lovely!" Mama beamed.

Kristin ran to the mirror and thought she was looking at a princess wearing the most exquisite string of pearls she had ever seen. She felt wonderful, as though a fairy had magically brought Grandma's hugs back. Her neck tingled and her head felt light. She just had to show her friends!

Kristin ran over to Mama, giving her a quick kiss on the cheek, and then tore away yelling "Bye, Mama! I'm going to show Melanie and Ashley and Kayla and Meghan and Katie…"

In the distance, she thought she heard Mama reminding her, "Be careful!"

Six

Kristin scooted out of the house. Her brothers were playing trucks in the front yard. Kristin nearly tripped over them in her excitement.

"Look!" she yelled as she flew past them, pointing to the treasure around her neck.

"Huh?" said Justin. Geordie ignored her, absorbed in the truck noises he was making.

"Never mind!" she laughed as she crossed the street to Melanie's house.

Melanie was very impressed. He mouth hung open as she sighed, "It's beautiful!" Together they went to show Ashley, who couldn't hide her admiration either. Then they played with Ashley's kitten for a few minutes, who batted at the glittery trinket around Kristin's neck.

"Oh, no you don't!" warned Kristin, finding a catnip mouse to distract the kitten. The mouse was a fine toy, though the kitten was convinced it was real. He stalked and pounced and captured his prey as though his next meal depended on it. The girls giggled at his clumsiness, and he soon was exhausted by his playtime. He curled up on Ashley's lap, wrapping his little gray body around the tattered mouse, and fell asleep.

"Let's go show my necklace to Kayla!" Kristin suggested, since the kitten was no longer entertaining them. They placed him onto a cozy pillow without interrupting his nap for the slightest moment. Then the three girls moved on to the next house.

Kayla "Ooo-ed" and "Ahhh-ed" when she saw the pearls gleaming around Kristin's neck, just as the other girls had.

"Imagine how it would look on one of my dolls!" Kayla suggested. Her eyes sparkled as she pulled her friends to the playroom in search of the perfect model.

"We could make this one a princess," Kristin said, draping the pearls over the doll's forehead, being a little careless.

"Or maybe a bride!" said Melanie, scrunching some white material under the pearls to make a veil. No matter what they did with the pearls, the result was beautiful. So beautiful, in fact, that they decided it was time to show Meghan. They scampered across the street. Meghan was outside doing tumbling tricks in her front yard. The four newcomers rushed to join her. Kristin noticed that the tiny string of pearls began to feel somewhat sticky and itchy on her neck. She thought her hair might get caught as she did somersaults and cartwheels, and perhaps she should take it off and put it somewhere safe. But her hair did not get caught, and she did not take off the tiny string of pearls. Or did she?

When the girls tired of gymnastics, they started on their way to Katie's. Suddenly, Kristin realized she no longer wore her tiny string of pearls. Her hands shook as she held her bare neck. When had she taken it off, and where?

The girls never did make it to Katie's house. They ran back the way they had come, following every step they had taken, searching and scouring. But no one could find the necklace.

Kristin trudged home with a sick stomach and a gloomy heart. First it was Ginghy, and now the necklace! Grandma's special treasure gift, like the hugs Kristin so missed, was gone!

Seven

Kristin snuck upstairs to her bedroom when she got home. She slid past the bathroom where she heard Mama singing with the boys as they splashed in the tub. She couldn't tell Mama about her loss now; maybe she would in the morning.

"Kristin," Mama called, "Make sure you take your necklace off before you go to bed."

"I will, Mama!" Kristin answered. A soft fluttering began to tickle her ears.

"And put it in a safe place!"

"I will, Mama!" The fluttering became a little louder. Kristin tried to brush it away, but it wouldn't stop.

Kristin readied herself for bed. She climbed between the covers, taking Ginghy and the empty box with her. Mama came to tuck her in.

"You must be very tired to get into bed so

quickly," Mama said. "Oh, look, it's Ginghy."
Kristin quickly turned the doll's face toward
her own so Mama would not see the crack.
Mama did not notice and kept talking. "How
nice to see her again. Are you all right?"

Kristin nodded her head firmly.

"But I thought you had homework."

"Mama, I'm so tired. Can't it wait?" Kristin
managed to whisper, barely holding back a
sob. The fluttering seemed even louder, like a
big cat purring. How could Mama not hear it?
But Mama just kissed Kristin on the nose.

"Well, since you have a big day tomorrow, I
guess your homework can wait. Good night,
sweetie." She smiled as Kristin cuddled the
box and Ginghy, and left the room.

Tears began to form in Kristin's eyes, making
big lakes under her thick lashes. What was she
going to do? She blinked, sending nine shimmering tears down her cheeks. Then, in the
hazy darkness of her bedroom, the fluttering
noise mysteriously took shape, becoming nine
enchanted little fairies with sparkling wings.
Kristin watched in wonder as they flew lightly
beside her face. Each gently lifted one of her
tears and soared off into the moonlight. With
the sting of her tears gone, she drifted easily

into a deep slumber.

Through the night, Kristin dreamed about the fairies and their moonlit flight. They soared about, deftly cracking each tear like a crystal egg, leaving a comet's tail of shimmering sparkles to drift sweetly to the ground, dappling the blades of grass with a million glimmering pearls of dew. The wind waited quietly while the fairies inspected their handiwork for the most gleaming, the most beautiful, the most perfect of the pearls. They each collected a favorite one, with the ninth fairy collecting two. Then, using strands of their golden hair, they made another tiny string of pearls as lovely as the first. When they were finished, the wind began to blow, just a gentle, swirling breeze, stirring the leftover pearls. The jewels trembled and were lifted into the air in a soft, circular motion. And on the wind was a song, distant and low:

"Hush-a-bye, don't you cry! Go to sleep little baby…"

Grandma's song! thought Kristin.

As the music faded into the darkness, the whirling breeze collected itself into a wisp of glitter dust that twirled up to the sky, and disappeared into the heavens.

Eight

Kristin awoke, delighted by the dream. She hoped desperately it was true. It would be a miracle if the necklace were returned to her! She hesitated, took a deep, hopeful breath, and slowly opened the box. The sick feeling returned to Kristin's stomach. The box was empty.

"Happy birthday, ten-year-old!" Mama danced into the bedroom and gave Kristin a "good morning" kiss. "Kristin," Mama stopped, seeing Kristin's somber face and the empty box in her hand, "what's the matter?"

Kristin had been pressing her lips together and scrunching up her nose trying not to cry. Mama's words let the sobs come rushing forth.

"Oh, Mama, look what I did to Ginghy!" Kristin confessed, holding the doll out for her mother to see. "And...I...lost...my...necklace!"

Mama's arms were around Kristin in a breath. She held her close, and Kristin cried. She cried for the loss of her tiny string of pearls, but she also cried for the loss of her Grandma.

"It's all right, sweetie. It's all right." Mama patted Kristin's back and took out a tissue to wipe the tears from her cheeks. Mama's eyes shone as she continued. "I think you are one of the luckiest girls around. Your grandma loved you very much, and always took care of you. And I think she still does. Look what I found in the rose garden."

From her pocket, Mama pulled out the tiny string of pearls, shimmering and glimmering, just as it had yesterday. Kristin held her breath in wonder.

"There is one thing I don't understand," Mama continued as she put the necklace around Kristin's neck. "I thought there were only nine pearls on this necklace, but today I counted ten."

Kristin touched each of the precious pearls, and sure enough, there were ten. Kristin smiled as she realized Grandma might be gone, but her love would be with her forever.

"I guess it's ten pearls for a ten-year-old!"

Mama said.

Kristin closed her eyes and held in her fingertips the tiny pearls around her neck. She knew she was getting the biggest Grandma hug of all.

Red

Written by R. Barbara Fay
Illustrated by Jim Stahl

shamrock
Publishing, Inc. of St. Paul

For our beloved dogs:
May we see the gentle wisdom in your eyes,
and may we treat you with the same
unconditional devotion you share with us.

One

Swoosh!

Zach's foot contacted the soccer ball at the perfect moment, giving it the full force of his kick. The impact felt good, strong and swift. His watched the ball soar in a splendid arc, clearing the goalie's fingertips by a good five inches.

"Yes!" Zach hollered as the ball torpedoed into the upper left corner of the net. "A hatrick!" he whooped, raising his fist and running wildly toward his nearest teammate. They slapped hands high and hard in the air just as the referee blew the whistle to end the game.

"We did it! We did it!" A mass of green shirts pounced onto Zach until all that could be seen was a pile of wriggling arms and legs and bodies energized by joy.

"Hey! Lemme out!" Zach's voice was muffled, but his excitement could not be missed. His heart pounded and he couldn't catch his breath, but he didn't care. They had just won the final game of the season, earning the top seed in the play-offs!

"Okay, kids, break it up." Coach Mercer peeled apart the pile-up after allowing his team a few minutes of playful celebration. "Let's be good sports. It's time to get in line to shake hands."

Brandon, the goalie, was first to line up, followed by Zach. Melissa quickly slid in line behind Zach and the rest of the team fell in behind her. They all held out their right hands and haphazardly slapped those of the losing team as they filed past, offering half-hearted "Good job"'s and "Nice game"'s. Melissa gently nudged Zach on the left shoulder.

"Nice going Zach," she whispered into his ear. He turned around quickly, missing the next hand slap and almost tripping over his feet. Melissa's cheeks were pink and her blue eyes were bright. Tiny drops of moisture sparkled at her hairline, much too delicate to be called sweat. Zach could feel the thick perspiration on his own forehead dribbling along

the arch of his eyebrow.

"Yeah, sure," he stuttered, wiping his face
with a dirty sleeve leaving a muddy streak
across his cheek. Melissa giggled. The two
lines started to break up, each team heading to
its own sideline for after-game refreshments.

"I'll see you at the treats," she said sweetly
as she trotted to catch up to a couple of other
girls who were on the team. Her blonde ponytail swung back and forth, still smooth and
glowing after four quarters of play. Melissa
played hard, but she sure didn't show it. Zach
wondered if she had jumped into the pile on
top of him; maybe it was her knee that had
jabbed into his back...

Zach watched as a dog suddenly ran to her
from the sidelines and rubbed against her legs.
Its coat hung in brownish clumps like wet
ropes dangling from the end of a dirty mop.
As the dog wove back and forth begging for
attention, Melissa grimaced, as though the grit
against her calves was painful. She shoved the
dog aside in a way that made Zach flinch.

"Three to two, Zach! Three to two!" Brandon
came up from behind and proudly punched
his younger brother in the shoulder, the sharp
pain startling Zach. "What are you doing,

man? You're face is all red…"

"Nothing… nothing," Zach answered, self-consciously rubbing his face again, spreading the dirt more evenly. "Have you seen that dog before? She doesn't belong to Melissa, does she?"

"That old mutt? I doubt it. Melissa would have a poodle or something like that!" Brandon laughed.

"She's not a mutt. She looks like an Irish Setter."

"Whatever. I've seen it hanging around the field the last couple of games. I didn't think it could get any dirtier, but it sure has… just like you! You're a mess! Mom's gonna kill you, but she'll get over it you because you are a hero! We never could have won without you!"

"Nah," replied Zach, trying to control the huge smile that gave away his delight. "Anybody could have done it."

The dog looked up abruptly as though Zach had called her name. She eyed Zach curiously and cocked her head. Her gaze held his for several seconds.

"Hey, girl," Zach whispered, charmed by her deep, warm eyes. He took one step toward her, reaching out his hand. But she seemed

wary. She quickly turned and disappeared into the bushes at the edge of the soccer field.

Two

Zach woke up the next morning with an uneasy feeling.

What have I forgotten? he wondered.

Last night had been great. The whole team went out for ice cream and everyone congratulated him. Mom and Dad were proud and even Brandon could have burst. Zach was rewarded with a double scoop of his favorite ice cream, chocolate chip cookie dough, and he didn't have to share. Everyone wanted to sit next to him, all of the guys at least. And Melissa kept looking at him, smiling from the other side of the restaurant. She had never paid him attention before and he certainly had never paid attention to her. But it sort of made him feel tingly every time he caught her eye. Thankfully none of the guys noticed.

Maybe the dog was bothering him, the poor

thing obviously did not have an owner who cared. There was something strange about her, as though when she looked at Zach, she had known him forever. But that was a comfortable strange, a peaceful strange, not an unsettling strange. So why did Zach wake up feeling so awful?

Oh no! The social studies test! Zach suddenly remembered the unit test was today and he was supposed to have studied. Social studies was too hard: all of those details and all of those words. Words that didn't make sense; words that were impossible to read. Words like energy and employment and excavate. They all began with an "e" and had a bunch of letters... How could anyone keep them straight? Zach's stomach began to hurt. He laid his head back and shut his eyes.

About fifteen minutes later, his mother came into his bedroom.

"Come on, Zach. Wake up! You're going to be late!"

Zach moaned. He let his face fall into a pitiful frown.

I don't feel so good."

"How can that be? You were fine last night," Mom replied, her forehead wrinkled with con-

cern.

"I think I have a temperature," Zach said.

"Everyone has a temperature, Zach. You mean you think you have a fever?"

He nodded weakly. Mom brushed his hair from his forehead and felt his cheek.

"Hm," she said skeptically. "You don't seem warm to me."

"Well actually it's my stomach." Zach tried to force a burp for special effect.

"Zach, you must have had too much excitement last night and too much ice cream. Now get up and have some toast for breakfast. I'm sure you'll be fine once you're up." Mom pulled Zach's covers back and then roughed his hair with her hand. "I have to get ready for work, then I'll meet you downstairs."

"Sure, Mom," Zach agreed slowly. He swung his legs over the edge of the bed and knew that he was doomed.

The social studies test was the first thing Zach's class did that morning. Some of the questions were multiple choice, and some were fill-in-the-blank. The questions were about St. Petersburg, a town in Florida. Who cares about St. Petersburg? Zach thought. It's a

million miles away. And what is that word?
Industry or independent? It doesn't matter.
Just write in "factories;" those make things,
right? And the next question, something about
economy or ecology... Zach couldn't get past
eco. "Fishing" sounds like a good answer.
Florida has a lot of fish. Then came the next
question. The t... tr... tra... Zach looked
around. Marty Holiday had already turned the
page and Jennifer Murray was about to do the
same. How could they be done so fast? Even if
Zach had studied he couldn't have kept up.
He decided he'd better hurry. Nothing was
going to make him be the last one done. Now
what could he remember about the article?
Practically nothing. He had read it during
school, he really had. But it just didn't stick.
Nothing ever stuck. Not math facts, not
spelling, not social studies. It got all jumbled
up, like his dresser drawer when he couldn't
find his soccer socks. Zach saw Melissa stand
up to turn her paper in. His pencil scribbled
furiously as he rushed to finish the test. There
was something about old people... and Disney
World is down there too. Sure. Mickey Mouse
sounds like a good answer. There. Done.

Zach rushed up and turned his paper in

right after Melissa. He was the fourth one done in the class!

"I can't believe I finished before you did, Zach," Melissa whispered. "You're always done before me!"

Zach shrugged. "Yeah, well... you know."

This was not the first time Zach had thrashed his way through a test. Unfortunately, his papers usually came back from the teacher splattered with red correction marks as though they had suffered a gruesome bloody death. Melissa thought he was smart. What she didn't know was that Zach had a graveyard in the back corner of his desk stuffed full of quizzes and tests scrawled with red pencil. His failing marks screamed, "Zach Michaels is stupid!"

Three

Mrs. Campbell, Zach's teacher, was all too efficient that day. She had the social studies tests corrected and returned before the class came back from lunch. Zach gulped when he saw the tests placed neatly face up on each desk. Even from a distance he could see his paper covered with red marks, like a kid with chicken pox. He hustled to his desk and quickly stuffed the test into it.

"What'd you get, Zach?" It was Melissa. Her eyebrows and nose were scrunched as though she had seen something disgusting.

"Oh, I don't know," he stammered.

"It looked like a sixty."

"Oh, no, I think it was a ninety," Zach replied. He lifted the lid of his desk and took a peek. It was a sixty, and next to the numbers was written in bright red capital letters: SEE

ME!

"Yep," Zach assured her. "It was a ninety."

"No it wasn't," Melissa said. "I just saw it. It was a sixty!"

"Well, who cares?" Zach responded, slamming his desk shut.

"You're right. Who cares? Grades don't matter if you want to clean toilets for a living," Melissa hissed.

The whole class was suddenly quiet.

"I'm not going to clean toilets," Zach whispered, squinting his eyes in anger. "I'm going to be a pro soccer player. Pro soccer players don't care about St. Petersburg. And when you come for my autograph…"

"That'll be the day," Melissa retorted. She spun away from him, her ponytail whapping him in the face, and returned to her desk. A couple of girls giggled.

Mrs. Campbell walked into the room. "Class, get to your seats and open your math books to page 85." Zach was relieved to have the attention taken away from him. "This is a pop quiz to see how well you have been keeping up with your math facts." Zach's relief quickly vanished. It had turned out to be a *very* bad day. "You have fifteen minutes to complete the

forty problems. There is to be no talking. As soon as you get a pencil and paper you may begin."

Zach could not concentrate. He was boiling. Why should he care what Melissa said? Two days ago it wouldn't have bothered him a bit. What made her so smart? Never mind she probably got the best grades in the class. He had fooled her, hadn't he? And the rest of them. No one knew that he was just scraping by. No one knew that every word he read was a struggle and that he often had to do his math problems on his fingers. Pro soccer players don't need to know how to read. They just need to know how to kick and kick hard. *That* Zach was good at. He'd show Melissa and the rest of them. He'd show them at soccer practice this afternoon.

"You have five more minutes," Mrs. Campbell interrupted Zach's thoughts.

He took a deep breath. Oh no. Here we go again. He had only finished ten problems so far. Zach hopelessly completed the remaining thirty questions filling in any old numbers just to get finished.

Zach was anxious for the schoolday to end. When the bell finally rang, Zach was ready to

explode from the building with the rest of the class but Mrs. Campbell stopped him at the door.

"Zach, we need to talk," she said, resting her hand on his shoulder. "Let's sit down for just a minute."

"But I have soccer practice."

"It'll be just a second. Come sit next to my desk."

Zach slumped into the old wooden chair beside the teacher.

"Zach, you seem to be having more and more trouble with your schoolwork." Zach chewed at the edge of his fingernail and looked out the window behind Mrs. Campbell's desk. "I am very concerned. We are starting to get into some very difficult material but you are still having trouble with the basics... Zach, are you listening?"

He wasn't. A flash of brownish-red at the edge of the schoolyard had caught his attention. There it was again! As it came closer, he could make out the scraggly red hair and the slender frame. It was the Irish Setter! She was trotting back and forth with her nose to the ground, tracking in the direction of Mrs. Campbell's window.

"Uh, sure," Zach replied, looking at Mrs. Campbell squarely, trying to keep his eyes from wandering back to the dog. The Irish Setter stopped suddenly about fifteen feet from the window and sat down. With her ears perked up and her tongue hanging lightly from her mouth, she looked as though she were smiling. Her tail waved back and forth against the schoolyard pavement, sending pebbles scuttling in both directions.

"Have faith, good friend," Zach heard, the voice warm and caring. Zach sat up straight, startled.

"Huh? What did you say?" he asked Mrs. Campbell.

"Nothing, Zach. I was just wondering if you were listening," she replied. "Are you all right?"

"Yeah, sure." Zach fidgeted. The dog hadn't moved.

"Zach, I want to help you, but you have to try. You can't even pay attention to me for five minutes. Now, here is a note for your parents." She handed him a folded piece of yellow paper. "They need to know what is going on and I have a feeling they don't." Zach thought about the piles of papers in his desk. She was

right. He only brought the good ones home. He took the note from Mrs. Campbell and slid it into his backpack.

"I better go now. I'm going to be late." Zach stood up and flung his backpack over his shoulder. The dog stood too and leapt playfully, beckoning Zach out. Zach smiled.

"I hope to hear from your parents soon," Mrs. Campbell said, standing up also. "You know, Zach, soccer isn't everything," she added.

"I know," he admitted, "But it sure beats cleaning toilets!"

Four

Zach strode as quickly as he could out the
classroom door and down the school hall
without breaking the "No Running" rule. He
charged out the main entrance with hopes of
finding the strange dog in the schoolyard
when his foot caught on something sprawled
on the second step. The dog and Zach yelped
at the same time as Zach tumbled onto the
concrete and skinned his knees.

"Oh, man!" Zach moaned, rolling onto his
back. The dog came to him and made a soft
noise in her throat. She nuzzled his ear with
her wet nose. "What're you doing, girl? I did-
n't see you there. You're going to get us both
killed lying on steps like that." Zach reached
up and rubbed behind her ears. The burrs
caught in the thick mats pierced his fingers.
"Ouch! You are loaded with prickers! You poor

thing." Zach sucked on his fingertips. "Geez, first my knees, now my fingers. Just leave my feet alone. I'll forgive you as long as I can still kick a soccer ball!" The dog nudged Zach again. He sat up and wrapped his arm around her shoulders. Her shaggy coat was rough and the hidden burrs prickled through his shirt to scratch his skin. "Poor thing..." he said again. While he hugged her, he noticed a folded yellow paper being swept away by the breeze.

Oh shoot! The note! It must have flown from his backpack when he fell! The breeze carried it only a few feet when it slapped against the thick bark of the big old oak tree in front of the school. It unfolded and fell to the ground, inviting Zach to read it.

Mr. and Mrs. Michaels,

That much was easy. Mrs. Campbell's careful cursive was like reading a textbook.

This first month of school has been very

d...d...different? No—

difficult for Zach. His

under...

understanding of the basics is very poor. This year

requests? No, re... re...

requires a good working

know... know... knowing? and ut... ut... oh, skip it,

of basic facts which Zach does not have at this point. If we do not get a

han...

handle on this

sit... sit-something

very soon, there is no

dob...

doubt in my mind that he may need to repeat

REPEAT!?!...

this year. I

rec... rec... something...

that we test him for learning

dis... whatever... such as blah, blah, blah...

Zach put the letter down. Repeat this year? He could not imagine. He had just started and they already wanted to fail him? Repeat this year?

Zach sat down beside the tree and pulled his knees up to his chest. He shut his eyes and let his head rest against the jagged bark. Now he knew why he had had such a stomach ache this morning. The dog rubbed against him. She licked at his hand, then jabbed at his arm with her nose.

"Hey Red," Zach said. "I guess you have had it pretty bad too." Her ribs showed through her thin coat like a mountain range. Her tail wagged and her cheeks pulled back into that smile again as Zach petted her long body as though she were the most beautiful animal alive.

Zach carelessly refolded the note and stuck it into his backpack. He pulled himself up, brushing off his knees and the seat of his pants. Holding his head high and with the dog at his side, he strode all the way to the soccer field.

"Where you been, Zach?" Brandon called from the field. Zach dumped his backpack on the sidelines and ran out to sit beside his brother. The team was scattered about, arms and legs spread in various stretching positions.

"That'll be fifty push-ups, Mr. Michaels," Coach Mercer knocked on Zach's head. "Even the best players can't be late for practice. They need to be here just like the rest of the team." Everyone else was done with warm-ups and lined up for a dribbling drill. Brandon stayed behind and chatted while his brother sweated his way through the push-ups.

"How come you're so late? And what hap-

pened to your knees?"

"I had… to talk… to… my… teacher… and… then… I… tripped… over… the… dog… nineteen… twenty…"

"What dog?"

"Twenty-two… twenty-three… the one… from… last… night…"

"The disgusting one?"

"She's… not… disgusting… thirty-three… she's… actually… really… cool… thirty-six… She… walked… with me… to… practice…"

"I don't see her. Where'd she go?"

"Forty-three… over… there…" Zach motioned his head toward the sideline.

"There's no dog over there."

"Forty-seven… She's… right… there…"

Zach collapsed after his fiftieth push-up. He rolled over to point Red out to his brother, but the sidelines were empty. All that was left was the lonely dark green mound of his backpack.

"What'd your teacher want?" Brandon asked, no longer interested in the dirty dog.

"Nothing much…" Zach replied absently as he wiped the sweat from his forehead, scanning the park for any sign of Red. But she was gone.

Five

Zach grabbed a ball with the inside of his foot. He and Brandon dribbled over to the end of the line and followed the rest of the team, left and right around cones, sometimes making sharp turns and sometimes making broad turns. Zach lost control of the ball several times as a cone he hadn't seen would appear and trip him up. By the end of the drill he was breathless and frustrated.

"Line up for the two-on-two!" Coach Mercer yelled. Surprisingly, Melissa hurried over to be Zach's partner. The toilet cleaner comment still stung Zach, but Melissa seemed to have forgotten it. Her lively eyes were eager as she called to him "Let's cream this crowd!"

The two-on-two drill was a contest. Two teammates played offense and had to pass the ball back and forth while they ran the length

of the field. When they arrived at the goal-box, they were to boot the ball into the net for a goal. Then, one player hung back and played goalie and the other ran up to play defender for the next two players in line. Zach always won no matter who his partner might be.

The whistle blew and the contest was on! Melissa started with the ball and gave a good tap Zach's way. He scooted the ball back to her with no trouble. They were easily making their way downfield when Zach thought he saw something on the sidelines. He looked up as Melissa's pass flew past him and into the goal box. The goalie grabbed it and sneered "Gotcha Michaels!" Melissa said nothing. Their next turn wasn't much better. This time, Zach missed a pass high up on the field and the defender stole it away. The third time they made it to the goal box and Zach gave it a big boot but it flew wide to the right. The fourth time he decided he would get the ball to Melissa and let her make the goal, but his pass was short and rolled out of bounds behind her.

"You are hopeless!" Melissa seethed, no longer thrilled to be his partner. "Some pro soccer player!"

I gotta show her! Zach thought.

For their final turn, he was ready. Pass it to
me and back to you, back to me and back to
you. It felt good, easy, like it should. Back to
me, back to you. The goal line was in sight and
Zach was up for the pass. Melissa popped the
ball to him perfectly. He took three great
strides, brought his right leg back and thrust it
forward with all of his power. But he did not
contact the ball. His foot swung high and
missed the ball completely! Zach's legs flew
forward in the air and he landed with a dull
thud flat on his back!

The entire team was quiet. Once again, Zach
felt the eyes of all of his friends on him, just as
he had earlier in the classroom. He tried to
take a breath but his chest would not move.
Pain shot through his lungs as his muscles
pulled against the searing tightness. He could
hear some of his teammates snickering,
delighting in his embarrassment. His eyes
started to water and Coach Mercer was quickly at his side.

"You okay, Zach?"

"I can't... breathe..." Zach gasped, fighting
for air.

Coach Mercer rolled him to his side and
rubbed his back.

"Try to relax, Zach. Try to relax. You've had the wind knocked out of you. Just close your eyes. It'll come back."

Zach did as he was told. Slowly, slowly the burning in his chest started to cool. He opened his mouth and pulled in a deep breath of air. And then another and another.

"There you go. You're going to be fine. Go sit on the sidelines for a while until you're sure you feel okay."

The entire team had gathered around by now and watched Zach trudge to the sideline. Melissa looked at him as though he were poison.

"You sure you're all right?" Brandon asked. Zach nodded, leaving the crowd behind.

Coach Mercer blew his whistle. "Okay, kiddos, let's get back to practice!"

Six

Zach sat wearily on the sideline and began to think about toilet bowl brushes. He wondered which would work the best. Some had bristles that came right off the stick and some had bristles that came off a wire shaped like an "o." Some were made of wood and some were made of plastic; which would last longer? he wondered.

"You're pulling you're head," he heard a soft, little voice say.

"Huh?" Zach grunted, looking around. A girl was standing behind him, digging her toe into the grass. The tattered dress she wore was many sizes too large for her, swallowing her thin body in folds of faded fabric. Her bony arms poked out the sleeves then plunged deep into baggy pockets leaving only her knobby elbows to be seen. Her hair was tangled into

two untidy braids that sorely needed a brushing, but the color was stunning. What did they call it on TV? Mahogany? She sat down next to Zach, so frail she hardly bent the grass.

"You're pulling your head, Zach. You're looking where you want the ball to go instead of at the ball." Her skin was pale and under her eyes purplish-gray half moons sank above her cheekbones. She looked sick except for her eyes which glowed a deep amber-brown.

"And where did you learn so much about soccer?" Zach sneered.

"I know about a lot of things," was her reply.

"Yeah, sure. I bet I could beat you in a one-on-one," he bragged. His eyes fell to her feet. Her shoes and socks were badly worn and had holes that left her big toes bare. He felt sad and embarrassed for her. She seemed not to care.

"Not the way you're playing, Zach. I could probably beat you with bare feet and a blindfold on." Her tone was gentle and not at all boastful. She smiled fully, exposing a row of tiny yellowed teeth, like baby teeth that should have fallen out long ago.

"You're probably right," Zach admitted. "Hey, how do you know my name?"

"I've been watching."

Zach shrugged. Maybe she knew what she was talking about. "So what do you think I should do?"

"Keep your mind on the task first and then the goal. Control the ball, keep your contact light. The goal won't move, but your way of getting there might. You've got to have a good working knowledge of the basics..." Zach's ears burned. Had she read the note? His back-pack looked undisturbed. "...before you can master the goal. You're forgetting about the basics. So don't look so hard at the goal because then you will forget what you must do to get there."

Zach shivered. These words being spoken in such a tiny voice was very odd. How could a kid sound so... so... old? Maybe wise was a better word. They sat in silence for several minutes until Coach Mercer called to Zach from the field.

"Hey Zach, you ready to get your head in the game?"

Zach stood and gave his coach the thumbs up. He trotted onto the field thinking, work the basics. Coach Mercer passed a ball in Zach's direction. Zach watched it roll toward

him. From the corner of his eye he sized up
the goal about twenty yards to his right. The
ball rolled closer and closer. Zach concentrated
on his point of contact. He deftly caught the
ball with his foot, dribbled it three strong
paces and then kicked it with all of his might.
His laces connected with the ball and it shot
forth like a cannon, flying into the net.

"All right!" Coach Mercer yelled. Zach,
relieved, ran forward and pulled the ball out
of the net. He turned, wanting to thank the
girl, but she, like the dog, had vanished.

Seven

Zach's reading light cast a warm circle of gold around the head of his bed. The rest of his room was dark except for the faint glimmer of the stars and planets that decorated his walls and ceiling. The book he was supposed to be reading had fallen to the floor as it often did. Zach stared at the stars, too tired to read but not tired enough to sleep.

Mom had been very upset when she saw Mrs. Campbell's note. She had no idea Zach was having so much trouble in school. She wrote a return note saying of course Zach should have any special help he might need, and then she spent an hour drilling him with flash cards and spelling rules. Was this what his nights were to be like from now on? Thankfully, Mom hadn't done what Zach feared the most. She did not say he would

have to quit soccer. But she did say if his schoolwork didn't improve, soccer would be the first thing to go.

Zach reached for his book and thumbed through it, trying to find where he left off reading. The wind blew his curtains and the light rumble of thunder could be heard in the distance.

"Poor Red," he said to himself. "Where will she go if it storms?" A gust of air pulled a star loose from the ceiling and it twittered and fluttered and landed on Zach's chest.

"That's it," he said, as though the falling star was a sign. "I have to try to find her."

Zach pulled a sweatshirt over his T-shirt and slipped out the back door of his house. The night was dark except when breaks in the clouds let the bright moonlight shine through. Zach wandered through the deserted streets toward the soccer field.

"Here girl!" he called softly. "Here Red. Come on girl!" There was no sign of her.

When he arrived at the soccer field, his hopes were raised when he saw something moving in the far shadows. But it was not the dog. Before he could see any features clearly, he knew it was the girl from this afternoon.

She was kicking a ball around the field and having a terrible time of it. It looked as though she had never touched a soccer ball in her life.

"What are you doing?" Zach snorted.

"I'm playing soccer," she answered matter-of-factly. "What does it look like?"

"Not soccer, that's for sure."

"Well, give me a break. This running on two legs is for the birds!"

"Ha ha. Well maybe you better take up flying! You are awful!"

"Well, you're an awful speller!" she retorted as she tripped over the ball.

"But you made me think you were good," Zach reminded her.

"No, you wanted to think I was good. I just didn't say anything to let you know I wasn't." The girl patted a wobbly pass toward Zach, the open toe of her shoe catching on the grass. He hopped forward to receive it, then sent it back swiftly.

"That is why your mom is so mad at you, and Melissa too," she said, racing to recapture the ball after it zoomed past her. "By pretending you're so smart," she continued, "and by not letting them know that you're not always perfect, your mom and your friends feel like

you've lied to them."

"My mom is mad at me because I am dumb," Zach stated.

"Don't be silly. You sound like a quitter." The girl picked up the ball and bounced it from knee to knee, her legs getting caught in the fabric of her dress. "You know how you felt, seeing what a clutz I am? Your mom feels four times as bad because she loves you. She wants to help you but she can't if you pretend everything is fine. Only bringing home your good grades is like coming home after a game bragging about scoring four goals but not mentioning the other team scored five."

Zach stuffed his hands into the pocket of his sweatshirt. "Then what about Melissa? Why is she so mad?"

The girl bounced the ball off her head and chased it down. "I can understand rushing through your schoolwork so you'll be the first one done. It looks good and it feels good just to be done. But how many breakaways result in a goal? Not many. Melissa is let down because you made her think you were something that you are not."

"But she only likes me when I'm a star."

"Well then, that's her problem. It didn't take

me long to pick you over her. I saw right away
that you were the one with the kind heart."
The girl dropped the ball in front of her to
punt it, shooting it off the side of her foot right
into Zach's stomach.

"Ugh!" he gasped. "You trying to knock me
down?"

"Sorry," she giggled, her voice carried off by
a gust of wind. Zach tossed the ball back to
her, casting her a sideways glance.

"What do you mean, picked me?"

"Oh, nothing really. I can just spot a kind
heart from far away."

"And how do you know all that other stuff?"

She placed her foot on the ball and looked at
Zach.

"I don't know," she answered. A lightning
flash lit up the far-away horizon and the wind
blew through the trees in angry bursts. The
girl squinted her eyes and her hair fell away
from her face. She suddenly looked very, very
young.

"How old are you anyway?" Zach asked,
wondering more about this odd creature than
ever.

"In people years?" was her reply.

"No, in dog years. Of course in people years.

Or are you from some planet where the years are counted in seconds?"

"No," she giggled again, "but if I were, you still wouldn't believe my answer."

A bolt of lightning cut across the sky.

"Shoot!" Zach muttered. "That storm is getting closer. We'd better get home. I had wanted to find that dog—that stray one that's been hanging around. Have you seen her anywhere?" Zach and the girl headed off the soccer field to the darkened streets.

"Not lately," the girl said. "She's a sweet one, isn't she? But shy. She doesn't trust just anyone."

"I don't know," replied Zach. "She didn't seem to have any trouble with me."

"It's that kind heart I've been telling you about."

"Cut it out," Zach said.

"Really, Zach," she said, stopping him with a fragile hand. "It's your gift. No matter how bad things might seem, you'll always have your heart."

Zach shook his head. "Whatever." he grinned.

The girl fell silent and they walked again, more quickly as the weather worsened. Zach

called for Red but the sound was lost in the
roar of the coming storm. When they reached
Zach's house, the first big raindrops began to
fall.

"Do you want to come in?" Zach asked the
girl as they climbed the steps to his back
porch.

"Oh no, no thank you. I've really got to be
going."

"Where do you live, anyway?" Zach had
been afraid to ask. He pictured her without a
home, huddled in a cardboard box, cold and
lonely. He couldn't bear it.

"Oh, just a little ways over there." She
waved her hand loosely toward the sky.

"Well, geez, your parents must be worried."

"No more than yours," she smiled. "I better
be going before the rain really starts to fall."

"I'll walk you," Zach said.

"No, no," she insisted. "I'll be quicker by
myself."

"Well… okay. You'd better hurry!"

"I will!" the girl replied as she backed down
the stairs.

"See ya," Zach said as he opened the back
door slowly, quietly, to a darkened kitchen and
a sleeping house. He collected some leftover

food from the refrigerator and dumped it into a bowl. Then he found an old picnic blanket in the pantry. He brought them back onto the porch, hoping that if Red were hungry she might come to his house and find the food. He spread the blanket in a dry corner of the porch to give her a safe place to sleep. The lightning flashed intensely as the rain began to pour. In the brightness of the storm he looked up and saw the girl slipping between the reeds and brush of the field behind his house.

How weird, he thought. No one lives that way for miles. By the next flash of light, she was gone.

Red

Eight

The storm blew in, fast and furious. Zach crept to his bedroom, guided by the flashes of lightning and the glowing line of light beneath his bedroom door. The door creaked as he opened it, causing a lump in Zach's bed to stir.

"Brandon?" Zach whispered. The tuft of white-blonde hair poking between the covers could belong to no one else. Zach peeled off his sweatshirt and tiptoed over to the bed. "Hey, move over, bed hog," Zach said softly. "I need some room."

A sleepy Brandon opened his heavy lids just a crack.

"The storm…" he muttered, smacking his lips lightly. "I thought you might be scared."

"Yeah, yeah, I know. But can you make a little room for me?"

Brandon rolled to his side and yawned. Zach

crawled in beside him and quickly fell asleep.

A few hours later, Zach was startled from his rest. All was quiet; the storm had passed. Brandon was sleeping peacefully, comfortably spread across three-quarters of the bed. Zach's back ached both from his fall earlier and from sleeping scrunched into a corner.

It's better than sleeping out in the rain he thought, his worry for Red fresh in his mind. He got out of bed and stretched, milking away the ache. Maybe she's out there. Maybe that's what woke me up.

Zach tiptoed to the back of the house. He peered through the still dripping kitchen window onto the porch. The moon had set with the passing of the storm, and the night was black except for the glitter of tiny stars. Knowing there was no thunder now to muffle his sounds, he carefully twisted the knob to the bolt on the kitchen door. It unlocked with a sharp clack! but thankfully, the house remained still. He opened the door a crack and peeked onto the porch. The first thing he saw was the bowl of leftovers, now gleaming and empty in the pale starlight. He stepped onto the porch and over the bowl, wary of every squeaking board, and knelt down next to the

blanket. In the shadows, the blackness was almost complete. His hand reached for the blanket and was thrilled to feel the scrawny body wrapped inside.

"There you are, girl," he said, his voice smooth and soothing. He patted her back, comforted to feel her steady breathing through the fabric. His hands reached up to her ears which lay between the folds of the blanket. As he gently tugged burrs from the thick tangles, he thought about her rich brown color and what a beauty she could be if only someone would take care of her. "I'll brush you out tomorrow, girl. And maybe I'll give you a bath." His mind drifted as he continued to pull at the burrs, one by one tossing them over the edge of the porch. His eyes slowly grew accustomed to the night. He could make out the porch pillars, the rusty watering can and the broken wicker chair in the far corner. Had he not been so sleepy, he might have been more surprised when his eyes saw what he held in his hand was not the matted ear of the missing Red, but was the mahogany braid of the little girl.

Nine

Zach woke up in bed next to Brandon. How
did he get here? Was it all a dream? He was
stiff and his fingertips were tingly and
swollen, as though they had been plucking
burrs all night. He ran through the kitchen
past the suspicious eyes of his mother and
onto the porch.

"I picked up the mess out there, Zach," she
said.

"Oh, yeah, uh, thanks," he replied, afraid she
might be angry.

"Are you taking care of a stray dog?"

"Um, well, she sort of adopted me."

"Zach, you have to be careful. Stray dogs
might have rabies. And she might belong to
someone. Feeding her will only make her
come back here."

"Oh, she doesn't have rabies," Zach assured

his mother. "And I'm sure she doesn't have an owner." Zach didn't tell his mother that he was no longer sure she really was a dog. "I was hoping that maybe you would let me take care of her," he added, bracing himself for a certain "NO!"

"I tell you what," his mother said. "You catch her, then we'll take her to the pound. If no one claims her and if your schoolwork shows some improvement, your dad and I will talk about bringing her back to stay."

"Really?" Zach didn't know if he should be happy or not. He couldn't imagine Red locked up in a pound, or the girl for that matter. Did he really want to catch either one?

"Really," she said, giving him a hug.

Zach spent the day watching for Red. He looked out the classroom window between spelling words. There were forty of them; he wanted to be finished. When he started to rush, he heard a bark. He looked up and caught a glimpse of Red between the slide and the swings. Remember the basics. He slowed down, thought through each word, one at a time, and handed his paper in second to last. No one looked, no one laughed, and he actually got an eighty percent! He combed the play-

ground at recess, finding clumps of red hair caught in the chains of the swings. He left pieces of granola bar next to the school steps where she had lain the day before and they were gone before school was over.

At the soccer game that afternoon, Zach felt fierce. This was the first playoff game and he wanted to win! Right after the opening kickoff, he tore away from the pack with a stunning breakaway. Zach the hero! he thought, a double scoop of chocolate chip cookie dough ice cream dangling above the goal. He booted the ball, but he missed by ten feet! The goalie didn't even bother to dive for it!

"Loser!" one of the defenders from the other team sneered. Zach's stomach tightened. Amidst the groans of the crowd, Zach was sure he heard the little girl clicking her tongue. He expected to see her pale face and brilliant hair among the fans, but all he saw were the disappointed faces of parents and friends. And alone, near the goal, was a very disgusted looking dog. Red was here! She was laying on her chest as flat as she could, her ears low and her head resting on her paws. She barely raised an eyebrow as the goalie ran past her to retrieve the ball.

"Oh man, Red! I'm sorry," Zach sighed. "You would have to be here for that."

Zach had the ball again. He tried to forget about heroes and hat tricks and ice cream. The goal won't move, but your way of getting there might.

This time he slowed down. He dribbled to the outside then stopped the ball with his heel. He outsmarted the other team's defense with a tricky pass to Melissa which she promptly propelled into the net. The cheers from the crowd couldn't drown out Red's spirited bark or dampen her goofy doggie dance, her ears flopping and her tail wagging. Red's joy became Zach's as he began to understand what this was all about.

After the game, Zach declined to go out for some victory ice cream. Instead he waited for the crowd to leave, hoping that Red would stay. It was already twilight when he was finally alone, sitting patiently on his soccer ball in the middle of the field. The leaves on the bushes at the edge of the field rustled and parted as Red emerged and trotted over to Zach. She carried a stick in her mouth which she dropped with great delight at his feet.

"Hey, girl," Zach said, petting her in long

strokes, finding her much less dirty than the day before. "Wanna play fetch?" She crouched back on her front legs; her ears perked up and she seemed to smile. "Okay, here you go!" The stick spun through the air and Red raced to it, easily catching it before it fell to the ground. "Hey, you're pretty good!" Zach laughed as he threw the stick again. After four or five throws, Red slowed. She did not catch the stick, nor did she beat it to the ground. She laid down next to the stick and panted. Zach sat on his soccer ball and watched her.

"Where's the girl, Red? Is she okay?" he asked quietly. "I haven't seen her all day."

The headlights of a car flooded the field and a horn honked.

"Come on, Zach!" his mother yelled. "It's getting dark! Time to come home!"

Zach looked over his shoulder at the dog. Her glowing eyes cut through the shadows at the field's edge. "Dinner will be waiting, girl," Zach murmured. "Come and get it when you're ready."

Ten

As the days past, Zach lived with the hope of seeing Red. Each night, he placed the carefully saved portions of his meals on the back porch. In the chilly mornings, the empty bowl and the rumpled blanket, now often covered with a thin layer of frost, were a sure sign she had been there. There were days when he saw Red quite often and there were others when he didn't see her at all. When she appeared, it was usually from a distance and at times when Zach needed her most. When he wanted to rush through a math assignment, when he wanted to pretend to Melissa that he didn't need help with his spelling, when he wanted to be the soccer star no matter what the cost, when he was discouraged that Coach Mercer benched him for playing too rough: there was Red, sometimes smiling, sometimes sad,

always knowing with those clear deep golden brown eyes.

"Have faith, good friend!" The words would echo in Zach's thoughts.

Zach found himself changing, becoming more confident and more careful. Red changed also: her coat was now lush and her body had grown stronger. Zach wondered about the girl. If she appeared again, she would be stronger too. She would glow just like Red. Zach was sure of that.

"Getting ready for winter, aren't you girl?" Zach would say, running his fingers through her thick, gleaming fur on the rare quiet moments that she sat beside him. And then the two would play fetch, six throws the first day, ten the next, then fifteen or even twenty until finally it was Zach who grew tired first.

The season changed from early to late fall. Brightly colored leaves still decorated many of the oak trees surrounding the soccer field, though gray skies and heavy clouds signaled the coming of the first snowfall. Soccer season was over; the ground was hard and hurt badly if fallen upon. Zach and Brandon went to the soccer field for one last run around the goals.

As they jogged, their breaths created great puffs of steam and the first snowflakes started to fall. They were big and soft and cottony and quickly covered the field with white. Brandon was cold; he wanted to go home.

"Go ahead," Zach said. "I'll be coming right after you. I just want to look at the field one more time."

Brandon left and Zach looked over to the far goal. There she was, just as he had expected. She was magnificent. Her coat shone a brilliant mahogany against the flawless white of the snow. She sat tall, her head held high.

"I have to go now," Zach heard in his mind.

"I know," he said, swallowing against the ache in his throat. "I know."

"You're fine, now Zach. You've always been fine. You have a heart of gold."

Zach nodded. "Thanks."

"No," said the voice. "It is you I should thank. You have given of yourself and look at me now!" The dog leapt effortlessly back and forth in the snow, showing off her sleek, well-fed body.

"You helped me," Zach said.

"No Zach, you helped yourself. Your gift was always there."

"Who are you?" he wondered, amazed by her beauty. "How can you be so... so... good?"

"The greatest good comes from well beyond. It is not mine, yet it comes through me to you," the voice said. "You are too young to understand that fully. In time it will all be clear. It is the goal, the greatest goal. It doesn't change, but your way of getting there might. And though it will no longer come through me, be comforted that it will always be there." Red's mouth fell open and her ears perked up. Her cheeks pulled back into her wonderful smile. "Just don't forget the basics."

Zach kicked at the snow. He did not want this moment to end.

"Throw me a snowball, Zach," she said. "Nice and high, like you mean it."

Zach slowly reached down and collected a handful of snow. He shaped it and molded it and rounded it into a perfect ball. He looked up and aimed for the farthest point he could see in the sky. The falling snow stung his cheeks and his eyes started to tear. He pulled his arm back and flung the snowball with all of his strength.

Across the field, Red took three great running strides and then leapt into the air. Her

body flew as though it were weightless, higher and higher, right into the path of the snowball. As she caught it in her mouth, her body glistened and tremored and sparkled. For a brief moment, the sky was filled with an explosion of twinkling light. Then all that was left was the silence of the falling snow.